AWARD

for

NEATNESS

Trevor

For Mr Murray,
who encouraged my nonsense.

Scholastic Canada Ltd.
604 King Street West, Toronto, Ontario M5V 1E1, Canada

Scholastic Inc.
557 Broadway, New York, NY 10012, USA

Scholastic Australia Pty Limited
PO Box 579, Gosford, NSW 2250, Australia

Scholastic New Zealand Limited
Private Bag 94407, Botany, Manukau 2163, New Zealand

Scholastic Children's Books
Euston House, 24 Eversholt Street, London NW1 1DB, UK

www.scholastic.ca

The artwork in this book is acrylic (with pens and pencils) on watercolour paper.
Typeset in Adobe Caslon.

Library and Archives Canada Cataloguing in Publication
Blabey, Aaron
[Pig the grub]
Pig the stinker / Aaron Blabey.

Originally published under title: Pig the grub.
ISBN 978-1-4431-7033-8 (hardcover).--ISBN 978-1-4431-7034-5 (softcover)

I. Title. II. Title: Pig the grub.

PZ10.3.B519Pst 2019   j823'.92   C2018-903988-4

First published by Scholastic Australia in 2018.
This edition published by Scholastic Canada in 2019.

Text and illustrations copyright © 2018 Aaron Blabey.
All rights reserved.

6 5 4 3 2 1   Printed in China   LFA   19 20 21 22 23 24

PIG the STINKER

Aaron Blabey

Scholastic Canada Ltd.
Toronto New York London Auckland Sydney
Mexico City New Delhi Hong Kong Buenos Aires

Pig was a Pug
and I'm sorry to say,
his personal hygiene
was far from OK.

Pig liked to get dirty.
He frankly was RANK.

His paws could be frightful.

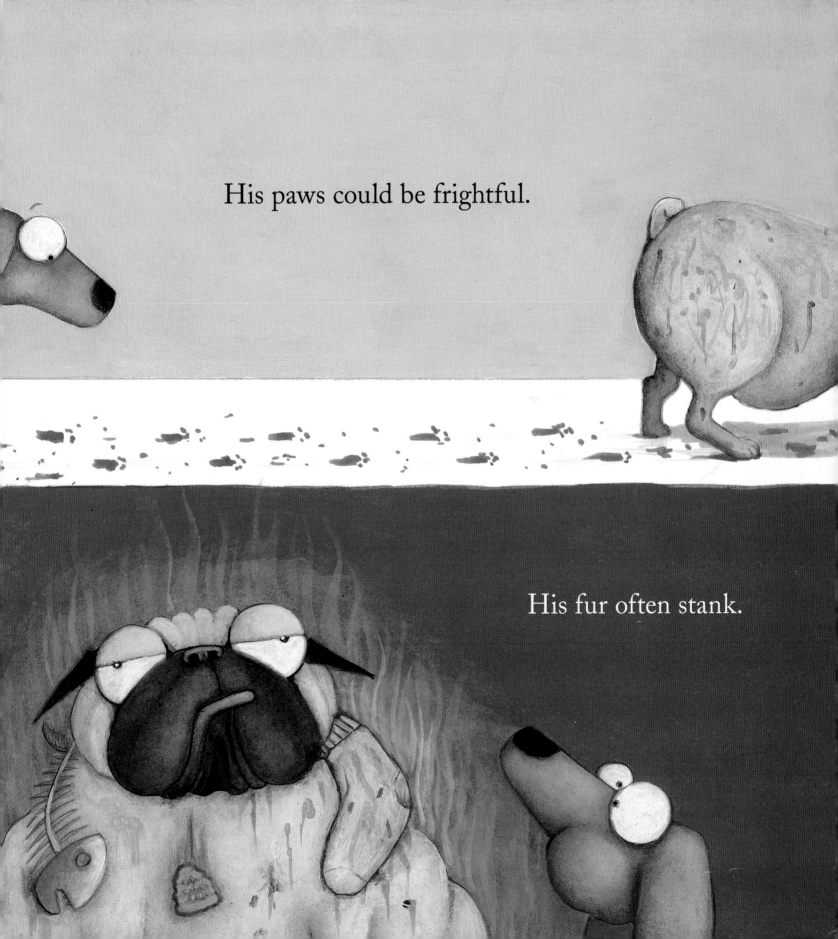

His fur often stank.

He wasn't offended
by odour or smell,

and if you weren't careful,
he'd smell you as well.

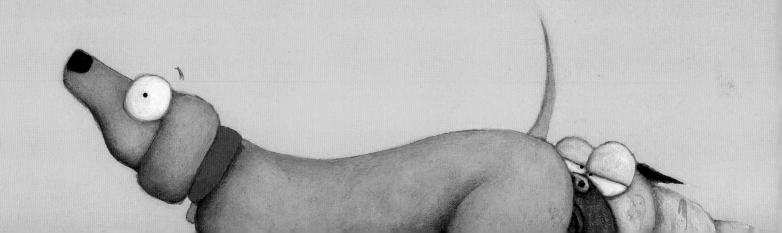

He'd play with all kinds of
unspeakable MUCK . . .

And do things to make you scream,

"DON'T
DO
THAT!
YUCK!"

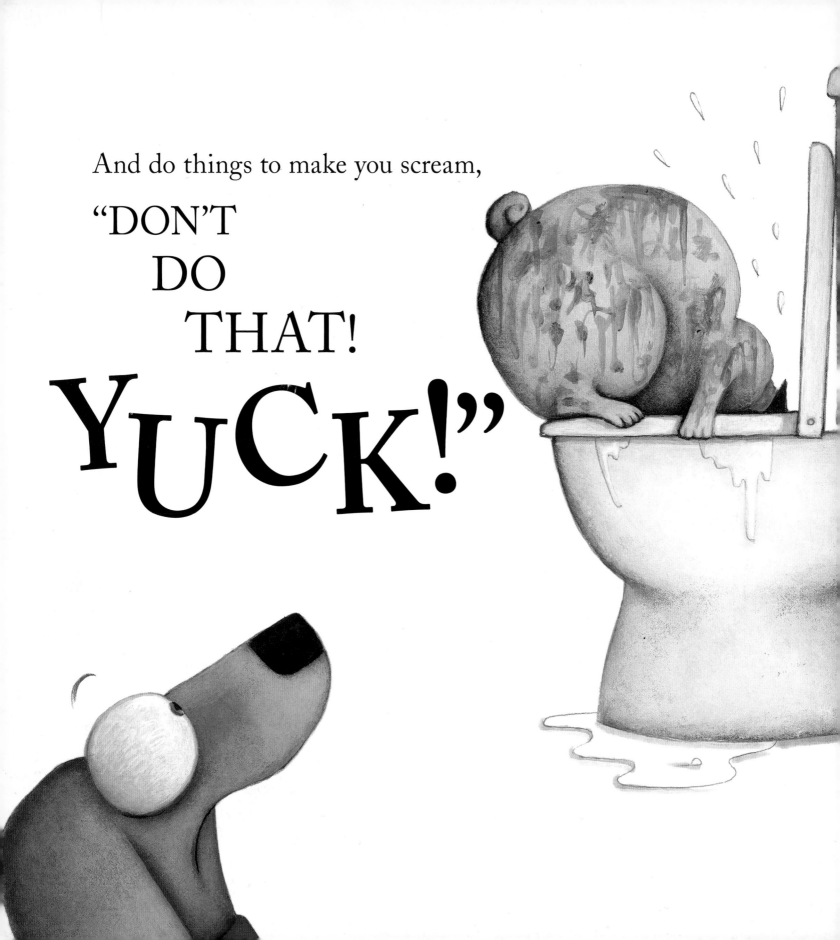

He leaked out a stench
that could not be forgotten.
He reeked. He was rancid.
In short, he was rotten.

So BATH TIME was called!
"You stinky old mutt!
You need a good clean
from your ears to your butt!"

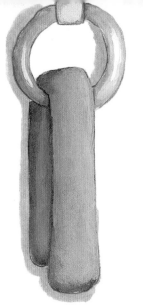

But Pig turned his tail.
And before you could grab it,

he was out of that room
like a foul little rabbit.

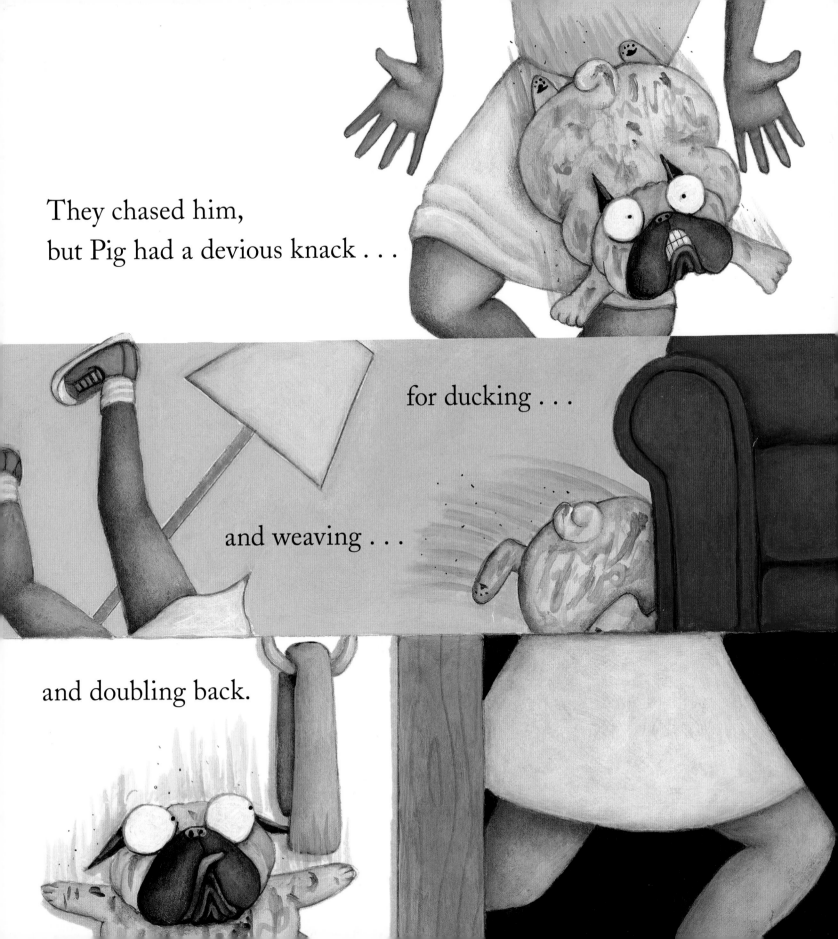

They chased him,
but Pig had a devious knack . . .

for ducking . . .

and weaving . . .

and doubling back.

And once he had lost them,
he used a small toy . . .

to block up the pipes . . .

then he hooted with joy.

By the time they had found him,
Pig boogied with glee.

"You WON'T GET
YOUR SOAPY
OLD WATER
ON ME!"

They watched as Pig gloated.

They watched as Pig crowed.

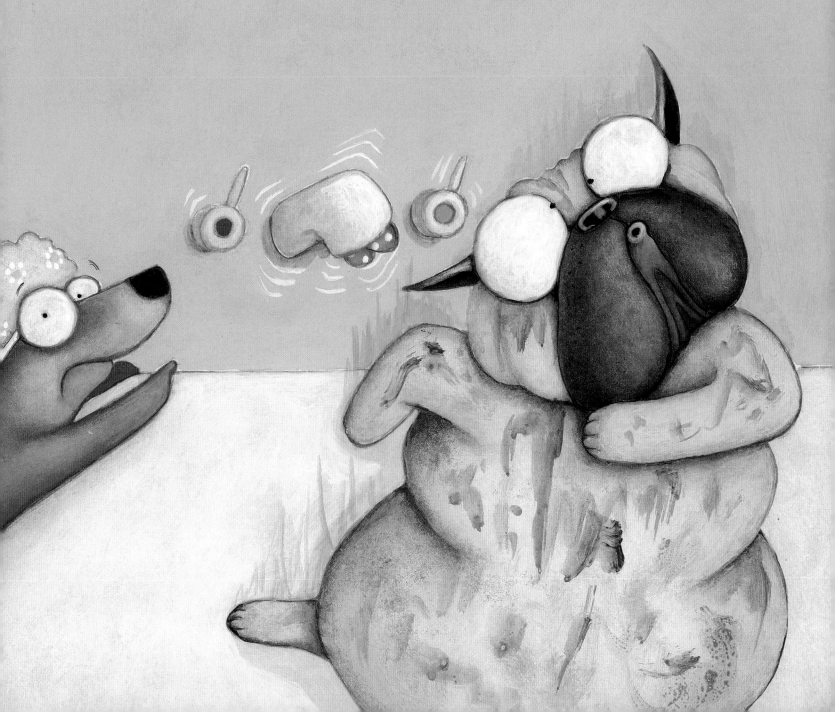

They
watched
as
Pig's
plan
made
the

bathroom...

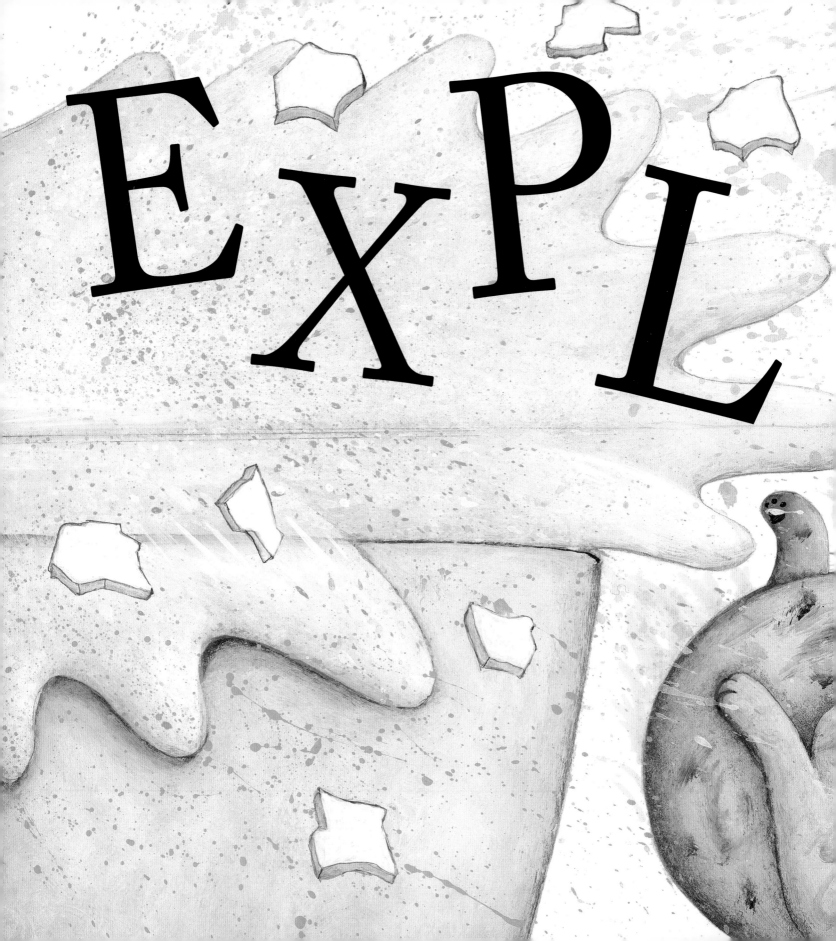

These days it's different,
I'm happy to say.
If you tell Pig it's bath time,
he won't disobey.

But although you can wash him
with soap, cloth and towel,
there's no getting 'round it . . .

DOG-E-BATH

Pig is just foul.

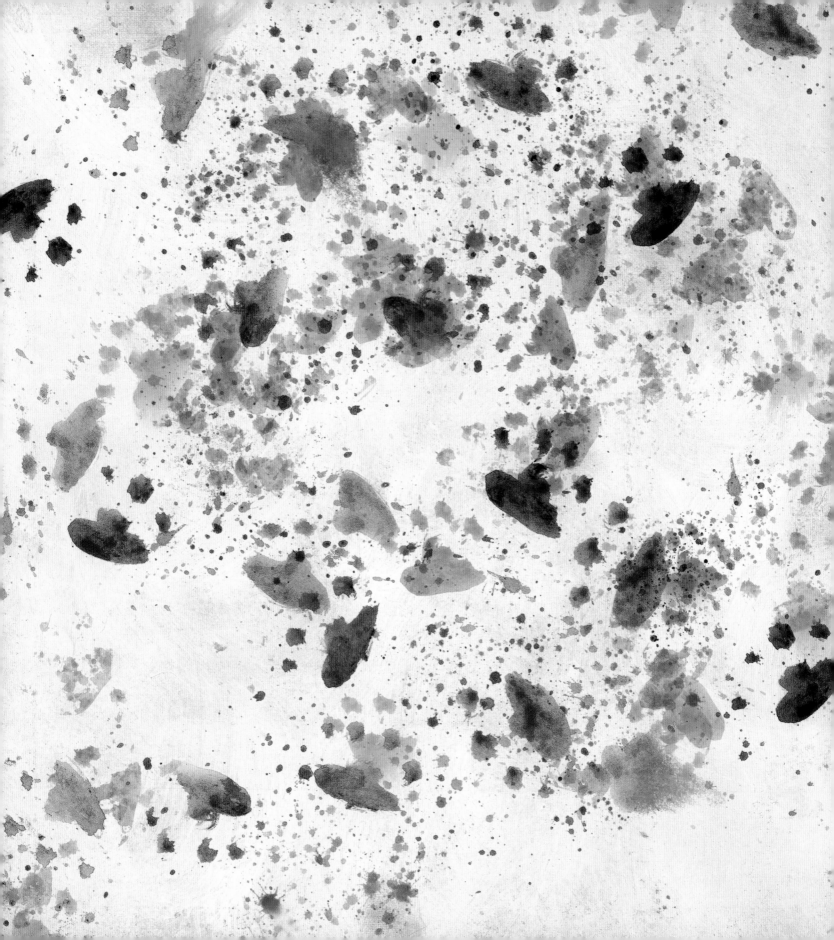